T0153287

Anselm Berrigan

Wave Books Seattle and New York

Notes from Irrelevance

Armed with an early
termination fee, a
delusion with regard
to neither denying
nor being of the past,
a lazy fly to center,
a transcription of
a stain on the soul
of the off-looker . . .
armless, disregarding
the mediated affect
of trees and their
privileged iterations
of objective fallacy in
the face of impassive
pregame nihilisms
tuned to talk's vanishing
outline, I came.
Having received visual

evidence of the life
I was meant to lead
I returned to writing
in a black and white
sketchbook in the
neighborhood where
I grew down to be
this writing in
accepted denial
of biography's tension
with anything less
than total capacity
for kindness on the
outside, the surfaces,
the skating conditions
across a version of the
present. But for living
only in passing in the
so-called country I'd
kill all its insect life.
I would. I'd do it
without spite or

resignation. I make no
attempt to grasp time,
nor will I shake off
being stranded in its
projected memory,
confronted as if in
a rush by a figure
returned from burial,
reminded of an alternate
family through its
partition, moving as
cheap matter through
the known angles of a
vast city fighting its own
rulers for the right to
generate surprise. It is
likely my kindness in
outward manner is a
conceit punishing this
ability to understand.
It's more likely I'm not
bent back far enough

to cast a glance your way.
Sweat is my sweetest
snare of vulnerability.
One drifts out of re-
cognition while the
body pushes another
body from shade to
shade. Have A Happy!
A Swisher's moment
of success drives a yes
out the bar to brood
merrily over a tone.
Then someone doubles
and anticipation's back
on the table. As forevers
go, the rock down is
remotely bearable in
terms of cosmic war
and beefy adaptations
of minor scrums in
tight-winged halo jobs.
The working folk are

feeling the economy
read itself out of
various long-standing
arrangements, con-
junctions need not
apply, but I'm not
feeling my compartments,
given the evil creatures
that inhabit their locks:
insert transcription of
NY Post here, fondle
inappropriate middle-
aged balls of pseudo-
conscious defense strategies
there. Hideki is about
as good a name as
Anselm. Carlos Berrigan
would have a certain ring
for umps on demand.
Our breed of scantily
clad harbor adrift in
concrete's sophisticated

open-headed blue.
When I get paid I
catch up and spend.
Brisk facet of hideous
self-assertion, why do
you dawdle on your
knees waiting for a
metaphysical paddling
no one will extend
from sheer commonality?
The baby sits on my thigh,
activates the cell's online
capacity by nuzzling
a pocket, spends money.
I buy her broccoli, sand
and shit intermingling
over cocktails in a sinkless
restroom that later
conjures childhood.
Shouldn't the distant
voicing of wisdom arrive
with dour passivity at

this point to instigate
the lab rats into gazing
at their withheld gazes?
She's got fried looks.
I've got a To Do list begging
for a million drinks. The
Tartar and The Venetian
contend in a stupor of
disquiet above the bitched-
out illusion in which,
along with a green slim
vase, I am constantly
hiding my torso in
front of our bloodshot
field of vision. Must
be carried out of this
overpriced vessel and
flung with innocuous
fervor at noise's wrecked
bounty. Sketch of a
neglected cinema: who
need be any way reshot

but the local tableaux
of desperate vanguards
and their unspoken armies
of flight. Cruising. When.
Those blue cats. Told
to never hear a word.
The dish awakens. I am
not inferno, no, no
matter how aptly
uncharacterized by
stranger and estranged
alike, my brooding bent
toward seeing, forcing
an issue out of perceptual
marginalia—“my life” or
more succinctly, my
humor. By now I am
forced to take this
surface seriously. Skin,
minor deterioration,
latinate pig fucker astride
a multichannel slint

of futures. I garble the
rhetorical aspects of
sensibility or silence
them altogether as
occasion implicitly
demands, to give my
child a chance to unfix
all she's told. I may
not be doing that.
Total retreat seems
inevitable for a parsec.
Elegance was a factor
at one point, havoc
in black tights firing
plasma circles at your
standard invasion. I've
not met an alien, or at
least every being I've
encountered has been
recognizable on one
level—who doesn't for
instance take their aura

of citizenry for a stroll
in some granite forest,
"some" activating an
emphasis on arbitrary,
which we of course
don't deal in here
mind you, unless by merit
of reflection, i.e., I *know*
I'm in the Bacon.
I don't have to have it
shown back to me. I
want to eat and be eaten.
There's no particular
mystery in that sense.
The generic rambling
passé mysteries of space,
time, friendship, filthy
rumination and little
curvy bends in the air
when the funeral
arrangements are being
made in two broken

languages and you
haven't slept because
you're heavier than
sleep for extended lack
of it, that's what I'm
eliminating "thought"
to handle. Blank is blank
is blank is blank. To be
scores and assumptions
an inked goddess did not
command, I bet against
my own aloof relations
with family, society,
labor and intellect. I've
mostly suppressed the
desire to compete with
everyone but myself, and
we are on a race to lose
most innately, with kindly
hostility to one another.
More saving. More moving.
A component of trust in

hand might be routine
for removing dated skin.
I am not most comfortable
removing layers of myself
at no one's behest. To
not pull vision off the
impact possible among
sphere, stick, and who's
gonna glove yr pretty
little hand, to not make
orders of oneself so
rhetorically abject.
My sense of my own
history with images is
such that I consciously
developed a willingness
to let them go—to not
take pictures though
I'd keep feverishly
those gifted to me. I
might like the feeling
a photo meant I looked

like something: vanity
to affect to desperate
preservation of a
moment that never
felt settled or even
moment-like. I've kept
hold of some shots
and now let fly an archive
online of pics other
peeps put up that has
very little to do with
me. This is a PG bar.
The tender does not
approve of our vulgarity.
Studying overload for
teachability feels a little
too now. The computer,
not the quesadilla,
told me about a moment
wherein my father,
talking to an old friend,
waxed nostalgic for a

moment they cohabited,
an extended moment,
and a fellow who heard
the rap from above got
mad and thirty-two years
later related his anger
in a comment box as way
of saying he couldn't
deal with the sadness
he perceives in Ted's
poetry. Is that a fair
judgment of a person
based on an overheard
remark to a then–
geographically distant
old running buddy
about how great they
were in their day together?
This stuff, I'm sorry,
moves too much, is too
heavy, you will have to
be replaced in order for

any of it to get caught.
Does the poet improve
her lot by working
harder to compensate
for the minor snuffing
of instinct? No. Does the
poet have a lot? I write
with the fact of being in
civilization as context
to which it is hardly
necessary to refer unless
some use gets cajoled
to the surface, making
plans to make plans
forming a foundation
for invisible suburbs
within the city. On the
question of influence
I seem to have forgotten
all the names, places,
objects, friends, failures,
experiences that might

make up the requisite list.
I at some point decided
to be—or became,
understanding later—
influenced by, potentially,
anything. Alignment with
lineage or historical arc
felt superfluous after that.
There are no conscious
connections within me
at all: my phone doltish
on purpose, all thinking
made of remarks, inhabiting
a borrowed consciousness
till human voices wake
me. I scare strangers
away by sidling up to
them and writing in
public. I don't really see
the difference between
modernism and Al Qaeda.
I'm looking to visit an

authorized dealer. I'm
collaborating with myself
on a mini Casio keyboard.
I'm going to make a list
of all the people who've
influenced me in any way,
with a brief explanation
as to how. Reality's frail
blooming is of no concern,
being only there. One
mirrors the dynamics of
massing without reason,
lies an honest, productive
lie, awaits questions. I got
my first real six-string to
play a flamenco version
of kibbles 'n bits. I was
taking the 12 or 20
questions seriously then
saw some potes of qualitay
taking them less seriously.
Impulses following include:

being more serious, being
less serious, being something
else, forgetting about it,
turning enemy, being
happy and free on a bike
in San Francisco ignoring
and or leaving the party
of thought. It's no small
thing to wish to abandon
thought. It's no thing, in
fact. But it's hard to talk
about when talking is one
of your vessels for thinking.
True loneliness, for me,
is being in a room full
of thinkers too busy to
listen to me answer their
questions, which I am
dying for want of being
asked. As currently one
of the six billion-plus
I must say that meaning

is not difficult to find;
in fact, being a poet and
generally oversensitive
sonuvabitch prone to
cathartic self-retaliation
at perceived slights while
maintaining a surface of
competent if protean
functionality, I find
meaning to be constantly
on the offensive, attacking
my desire to get going
and be a responsible
citizen in terms of hours-
on-the-job with their
seemingly effortless
reminders of intent
(though I don't give a
rat's ass about hours
on the job, as my
former employees can
attest, so long as they

aren't destructively
fucking about). I'm not
talking about big-picture
meaning, which is for
weakness, but micro-
meanings, the fact that
that tick means to bite
you behind the knee and
suck a little blood out,
not giving a shit it's
been on a deer all night
and is likely going to
make you ill as all hell,
a sickness meaning with
ruthless intent to recast
you as quite alive. I was
thinking about a singer
and a few days later her
song comes on and I
feel just as damaged
and lulled by its make
as I did when I was

twelve and the tune
was new, a hit, sax solo,
public-lipstick-on-teeth-
wipe-performance and
all. It has a timeful
empty elegance and
upscale pop sexiness,
and it's easy to sing with
while mock-seducing
your possible friends
into believing you share
a cool sensibility. That's
what I think, now it's
over. The other day
I was imagining the
Marquis de Sade,
pronouncing the Sade
part with additional
invisible letters: an h
after the s and an r
after the a. There would
also be pronunciation

of the e as if it were a
long a: the Marquis de
Sade, yes, I was only
thinking about the Sade
part: he himself means
nothing more than
opportunity, as all the
horrible pop songs that
haunt my chintzier memory
play all around me. It
doesn't matter, if they're
there, what they are.
Simple tics turning into
an evolution of practice
and, subsequently, a
survival guide to be
passed on to paying
would-be artists. I too
contain an adjectival
tradition of whoredom
already old by the time
I used it and have ten

minutes to write this
unless the roof caves in
and a gumdrop falls
in my mouth, in which
case I will have sold out,
thereby becoming more
for the people if not of
them in some second-
wave rip-off blues romp
articulated in tight-pantsed
outsized arrhythmic lips
consistently off a step so
as to be in perfect sync
with a brazen character
who will endorse your
every move from the
inside of a dilapidated
think tank wherein
further schematics are
plotted for the betterment
of your imagination's
wizened sincerity, and

that only took six minutes.
Is a nude picture of
Jackie O found in
Andy Warhol's suitcase
really a bizarre item?
Isn't it a slightly tone-
deaf piece of nostalgia,
an entryway back to a
simpler time when there
was less to know about
so much more? Or did
I get that backwards?
Shit. Too-much-ness
must be a domestic
solitary state if ever
deemed source of
inspiration, which we
are going to consider
in broad terms for
the purposes of this
impasse, data now
so widely available

as to be conditioned
unavoidable, not only
impractically ubiquitous
but its own selling
point. Who can avoid
taking part in this multi-
layered exponentially
self-generating existence
we drive forward,
participate in, are subject
to, at once, regardless
of our wishes (though
typically, it seems, in
abeyance to them)? In
that we're waiting on
the okapi to organize
and go on strike, or
counterstrike. In that I
am waiting for the stuffed
okapi, the evil kitty, the
frozen hop, the spineless
doggy, the tubby fox

with babe to organize
and resist. I don't think
the destructive will aimed
on the inside *is* elusive
if one *is* sensitive, but
the tangle of sentences
is hard on the eyelids.
Can we agree coverage
should diminish then?
Then. I didn't know her
fighting version. Signs
of virtuosity are no
impediment to the punk.
Alienation so badly
wishing to be seduced
into violence. Reserved.
Love of boxes, love of
being put in shopping
bags and swung in circles.
The recession's cut down
of bodies in public
commercial spaces is

helpful to me as I often
prefer to practice with
some but not many
strangers in the same
establishment. I like
to pay for time as I go
or am just used to doing
so and currently willing
to remark upon it under
the rubric of being
personal, though it's
just as personal to wipe
my dirty hands across
these pinkened eyes or
pluck that bug from
my wine, both banal
gestures devoid of
disgust. Revealing isn't
being personal so much
as taking part in society's
desire to render each
individual as semi-

functional leveled body
of neuroses; of course
that's been true for
decades and I just got
raised into the scheme.
Borne by plastic
scheming and a desire
to process love, I held
the gauze of complicit
masturbatory friendship
and gave it a shaft to
embroider, to name,
to socialize in relation
to stuffed things bent
on providing nondisposable
comfort. I enjoyed
serving food, too, at
the Levee, the bar, the
deep-fried stuff. Fine
food and homemade
ketchup, I mean, I'll
eat an orange blossom

bolstered by history's
series of bedbug-
vanquishing strategies.
All you need is alpha
phi / all you needed
was clarity to pull the
plug / all you'll need
is an ability to hoard
the blackest nights and
put them to better
work for your ecstatic
unknowns—we are
the only ones available
to torment torment,
as you'll know if you
glimmer our caustic
wall remarks. I have
several vicious profiles.
I took the evil kitty twice
today without asking,
producing tears, then
tears and hyperventilating.

Tenderness toward
self-loathing and withering
angst don't seem to
hold out much promise,
tonally speaking, though
it's possible I need to
do something more like
recognize I start there
before turning it into
something else, and in
course, being a poor
specimen, between
mostly kind treatments
and mostly unmasked
arcs of characterization,
I stopped, somewhere
along this way, looking
for myself in others,
other works, my family
—a photograph would
attempt to prove
something, but surfaces

and the matter of dna
are no more than facts
to reorganize within
their frameworks of
brutal delicacy. The
incidental face mask
rule went out last year,
a failure as a rule if not
an emblem of gaming
contact. Solidarity has
been less than a myth in
our future imagination
I fear without reason or
its inbred resemblance
to active policing of
our collective desire
to be just free enough
to dull necessity. I
know, I know, we're
all polymorphous within
our relations to modesty.
I swear this won't take

long, no longer than
any other fantasy of
structure teased across
a daybook, a computer
screen, a workmanlike
routine of getting in and
out of the assigned places
of ass-to-seat interaction.
And yet I do not trust
the sanity of my vessel,
nor that of metaphor,
built across time to be
diminished by speed's
freezing of the body in
place, as like or so being
near to and no less
against while with and
in relation to being seen,
everywhere, or, more
precisely, anywhere.
The hope of a plurality
of recognition guides

us into, back into, our
common definition of
caring, if not cares. I
was busy always relaying
your time through
the disingenuous manners
to which I am lashed.
Facing a reboot harm-
onizing, for why would
a machine bother with
affect, much less one
bent on intimidation.
The psych profile
restrained, "secure in
torment." Unable or
unwilling to measure the
qualities of desire as we
stand in its relation, I
find I stare at your script
from afar, wondering if
the open, refined, sensuous,
conservative imagination

it projects is a functional
defense against the light
arts, or more of an active
missionary filter with, for,
and from reality's stance
on a version of "us."
Crimson elephant
smiling from a poster
for art disguised as
delirium. Does it nod?
It accentuates a variation
on self-destructive finish.
Well, fine. Flowers can
be traced back in ink
to a common glandular
pitch, posing as a pose,
speech dissected in front
of the face and thereby
unattended in the tear
open. Look. The problem
of assessment being the
regents exam of existence

in a less-than-slimy way,
and we need the slime!
Where is the function
of sleaze in relation to
my coddled measure of
sacrifice? It's uselessly
unhip to penetrate a
machine gun and leverage
a relationship with
modern consciousness,
which is a perfectly
devoured bug off the
hind leg of some
preserved thing. I have
buried deep within
my bypass a silent love
for the arch of your
fierce wistful squeak.
I would like to spend
time in a failed state
with your bending frame.
Something like an

unqualified interaction
was on the table just now
and while the decision
to discontinue said inter-
action was not remotely
difficult it is marginally
notable. I notice you've
given into apocalypse
fantasies in an open
fashion—I hope that
works out for you, being
a tad classier than
conspiracy lust and less
likely to wear down
your comrades in
sociability. I myself
have returned to the
civilized wasteland of
the novel, wherein I
begin to notice a need
for detached attention
to matters of will, sub-

jugation, and something
like desire though not
exactly. Desire strikes
me as routinely out of
sync with time in most
sentences, as if a creeping
desire, one that refuses
to lean on what it means,
has been abandoned
by sentence and image,
consigned to quiet
behavior that eats at
the self's duration despite
giving it flecks of purpose
to decorate the larger
aims of mind, whatever
those might be according
to one's ability to resist
being told how to think.
Couldn't the perception
of rules, order, tricks,
and brainwashing be

more sensitively addressed
in the public arena? Have
we not been raised to
believe we're being fooled,
so that to respond "rightly"
to such conditions means
choosing a side even
though to choose is to
consign oneself to a cycle
of perpetual anger and
defeat? One looks for
articulations that fit a
game of resistance—the
problem is in the looking—
I don't think it works to
plead for a voice out of
the monolith to make
clear what *you* sense, feel,
know to be happening.
Not "true." Happening.
I have no memory for
images, not much of one

at any rate, nor for names,
nor the riding details
of going place to place.
Bodies? Yes. The hope
of bodies? Yeah. But
mainly the memory of
feeling stays with me,
possibly causing pain . . .
well, maybe only when
truly incapable of being
less than illogical in
the face of confrontation.
As a fundamentally quiet
person capable of great
bouts of pouring forth
black and white riddance
of the very notion of
the unnatural, I yell on
occasion to reestablish
presence, to push my
voice back into a quiver
of no control, to get a

bloodier sample of that
violence against myself
which is my primary
hedge against treating
others badly. In that
sense I remain a middling
specimen. But I defy
the lens nonetheless,
and may very well spill
triumph onto its porous
backside for a public
laugh in the distant
so-called future. I can
admire a kind of
comparison at times,
the kind that ultimately
collapses under the
weight of difference's
brilliance and the hope
that we may remain
deeply unknowable
to one another past

shared flesh and wistful
ferocity of experience,
but that or that being
going a near part to
which of this by will
and in so far as scrum
scrum scrum . . . neither
pliable nor withering
calamity of gack. So the
task is to find a new way
to speak, to tell of being,
tell being to fuck off and
come back with a steelier
measure of lack, a kinder
spirit for company,
distance, pain, fortitude
in the empathetic grist
rephrasing caught rides
half the time, or so a
speaker badly sung
with snarling hook
intones. Having walked

through a drizzle of
known blocks to arrive
at a relationship with
the harpy's economy,
incised with perfumed
soap dispensed as cheap
disguise, I am most
certainly engaged to a
dissolution of image,
even as I wield my own
anti-program in glossy
fashion. I'm a child
programmed to punish
the world. No one will
believe this, but it's as
uncynical a thought—
meaning it provides
no defense for anyone
working against being
tricked—as I can deal
from the register until
someone pushes a lesser

button. The green lantern
hoodie looks applicable,
the real digital-like rain
feels applicable, the
throbbing mistlets in
dapper fatigues bumming
for tipsy change are
applicable in their
corollary vastness to
my primitive state
defined back to me by
blasts of pop in some
former dark Ukrainian
bar's cousin. O solitude
as public refuge and
backward tumble through
demi-historical banners
of Them Who Was Alive . . .
caring is a daily non-
chalance. I cannot be
your cannot be. Your
man. You didn't, ahem,

ask. These events in time
as a reflection of previous
events in a prior time.
That take doesn't account
for this amount of light.
Let imbalance tear me
away from the rendering
of joy? Having made
the choice to blow
off a lecture slated for
the time block of 2–4,
when I lead something
named Studio, on
grounds the lecture was
mandatory for all the
students but not for me,
I find myself walking
through Williamsburg,
Brooklyn, where I lived
some ten to thirteen yrs
ago, in an Italian pocket
by the Lorimer St L

station, feeling as if
some gnawing vitality
is sheathed in plexiglas
around me, and there's
the possibility of seeing
some neon reflecting
off the sheaths that
have a passing contour
similar to dust on a
contact lens mixing with
bastardized specks of light
pretending to signal an
acid recidivism, but that's
about as far as it gets, "it"
being my impulse to be
in some state of intensity
or drive that's rarely ever
been a true encasement
for my measure. I can
agonize in an ordinary
fashion over imagined
conversation with the

boss as well as anyone,
but in truth I have a few
employers without the
spectre of an actual boss
figure. This is a kind of
working situation I've
imagined and now more
or less achieved, but the
fact of an interaction
with an authority figure
as out of reach is proving
to be emptier than I
might have thought.
That's probably a point
of real stupidity on my
part, some haphazard
bus ride of fancy so as
to extend a sentence,
but there's at least a
germ of truth in there
infecting my psyche.
Then at an uncertain

register in the late
afternoon—a time
when my crumbling
may recommence in
a knowing fashion
that is never without
humor nor resigned
to variations on the
accents of fate—a case
is made to re-enter
a measure of grief, but
do I not already contain
uncodable degrees of
grief in corrosive images
rendered back at me as
an interruption of being
to be somehow grateful
for? As if lives plucked
from our scans of the
premises could steel us
up for the longer haul
more accurately depicted

by a series of idiosyncrasies,

scratches, quiet lousy

ethereal habits that keep

us at once within and

gleefully locked out

from the wirings, my

love, of life? Get a hold

of yourself General, for

the bugs' arrival is neither

imminent nor to be

feared. Let the heart of

the young be processed

by the heart of the old.

Let there be e-i-o and

plenty kitties. One way

would be to run some

guns / make some new

buds / give away a leg

& call it a day / Another

might be identifying

with faces in vases,

banishing their stresses

and ignoring the striking
wait staff dressed in black
and blue denim, that fabric
a steakhouse uncle's basis
for bonding back in Cali:
"So, you like denim?"
"Yeah." No response, nor
even any bits of speech
the rest of the paid-for
eve, a glimpse of well-
engineered suburban
depression mashed into
big-house living. So
what if it was disbarred
from dreaming. Another
way is friendship, the
trenchant ride or series
of curious demands and
nearness to the way you
feel drifting forward
along fourth street toeing
Marcella's orange line,

a find-your-way-home
painted path I could have
used leaving Eileen's
apartment at age eight,
forgetting I didn't know
east from west the way
I sometimes still put my
shoes on the wrong feet
not to mention Sylvie's,
and winding up stranded
in the dark of third street,
a block over from Hells
Angels' headquarters
and the residence of Mrs.
Roberts, compared
rather aptly to Vince
Lombardi by my father
though Sonja probably
had a slightly more
imaginative definition
of winning. Her meddling
attempt to convince me

boarding school was a
terrific idea—this
a tortured motivational
ploy the first day of
school; no wonder Dad
likened her to a football
coach—and though it
reduced me to tears, anger,
lying, and fragility in the
third-floor Asher Levy
hallway as she attempted
to convince me Ted let
himself die—her gossipy
misunderstanding of his
desire to go out in his own
bed two months prior
when his liver failed,
likely fed by poisonous
rumors circulating around
St. Mark's Church—the
whole experience was
less fearsome at its

present than the quick
evaporation of my city
compass leaving Eileen's,
until some kind stranger
approached and put me
on the first ave bus,
though not before loading
me up with powdered
candy for the five-block
ride to familiar terrain
on St. Marks Place.
Upon my shaky arrival
my mother was ready
to call Eileen and give
her the hard business
she was later to give
Mrs. Roberts after I told
her about that sixth grade
shakedown, but my father
said no, call Elinor, who
had taken me to an after
party at Eileen's for a

poets' theater production
of Joan of Arc I had a
bit part in as a newsboy,
call her because she'll
actually feel *guilty*.
Eighteen years later I
absolved Elinor of her
long-standing, much-
discussed guilt with the
words "I absolve you
of your guilt." One may
be so dispossessed as to
emit the frailest of leers
at these mood-lit
passersby. Who shall
commit their organs to
a solution of gold liqueur
and pigeon shit dispersed
as conditioned air with
a feeling for no inside
world, no groping of hands
within the rib cage? This

shortcut through projects
for the aged almost
tames a barely rendered
playground into an
illusion of use for those
pesky pigeon-feeding
bike-riding dogs! I will
not grovel ethically before
just what is. I will never
abandon my desire to
recede into and out of
interconnection just
because I can't help
spreading out in strange
places from some need
to be seen in my life in
the world alone. Diaper
fornication just wants
to be pure, to pay down
the card's balance, to
handle degradation with
style, to lie as safeguard

against complacency,
to wear the interviewee's
headphones between
innings, to slouch and
deliver until fading into
completion, to merge with
the enemy and absorb
its best qualities, to puke
in the corner and ask
for wipes, to love the evil
kitty and its scratchy
glass eyes, to give in at
every moment and keep
it perfectly quiet. Getting
some absolution out of
the way comes first,
followed by feeling like
a relic, then instant
blistering of self for
indulging self-pity
before another kind
of desire tickles the

psyche. That's one
moment. The next
slightly longer moment
consigns an empty hallway
to emblem of future.
Were one detached
enough to dismiss
operating from anxiety
in order to be a ruthless
collector of materials it
might work to combine
radical progress with
institutional acquiescence
in the name of movement.
Reading the *Times* by
neon green light in this,
my neighborhood of
delusive transisting,
cleaned up for double-
decker tour buses and
their radio-voiced waves
designed to make a

museum out of the dug
streets. I love the view
up first ave on a clear
day, a straight line north,
a wiped-out horizon
stood on its side to
appear climbable above
the ordinary hum of
death that is traffic. I'm
for Nero's spinning
party room and against
unmanned drones,
though I like the idea
of a manned drone,
which sounds like every
allegory for society I've
ever paid money to
view, yet the run-down
parallel jism tracers are
One in the thick of
authentic greenery no
longer natural. I canceled

all sense of class for an
afternoon just to impress
your penchant for casual
protosymbolic gestures
of deep irresponsibility
that secretly (not so)
afflict routine with
love's wilier feints.
Forgive me. It was time
to make a break for it
and honor a decade's
worth of complicated
walks. Cosmic intercon-
nection of all beings?
Check. Futility of pain
management as source
of humor in outlook?
Check. Controllable
vices for purposes
of a secondary level
of interior life, an echo
of conscience trailing

out? Check. A sense of
time as discontinuous
in its spread while simul-
taneously expanding
on a surface line that's
only a reflection of
a sense of a line?
Check. Total distrust
of command but for the
contradictory moments
of necessity? Half-check.
Digging the ecstasy
of swinging? Yes. Laughing
at the tree? Is the tree
funny? Yes. So what if
the rain is friendlier
than your ever-slithering
definition of work, or
the chip in your pocket
is merely a lifeline for
complaint superseding
the hardy constant tributes

life makes to acceleration
of everything but generosity
freed from the promise
of entering history as
readable image? There
are little cards offering
digestible portions of
the path with dressings
vouched for by agencies
of seamless repute. Yet
truth is in the uglier
cracks in one's own
facade, shrink-wrapped
into neglecting decision
on a most unflattering
scale. What is most
ordinary every day is
defeating the desire to
harden into respectable
indifference. And what's
nice about not drinking
is what makes that piano

feel, I mean thinking

less about dying, less

concretely at any rate

of interior exchange,

staring out at the grey

childhood haven of

New York in October,

and what's not so nice

about not drinking is the

desire to have a drink and

think a lot about dying

until my inhibitions are

defeated and I can react

quietly from a zone that

is enough of the cosmos

to let the lights be more

than time's progressive

memory, and it's necessary

to finally renounce violence

everywhere in one's life

but in one's self-accusations

isn't it. I bring anger

to the evenness necessary
to be reborn without
strangling the doc. An
unexpected benefit
from the genetic process.
Attention dissolves:
Brooklyn into two-
dimensional space.
Oakland into pig-think
frequency. Demolition
into elevator love triangle.
Symbolism into punk-post
appliance. Foraging into
withdrawal from public
action. Voracious coddling
into confidants anonymous.
Story fate into shrubbery
lashings. Backlash into
dispassionate textolatry.
Rummaging into structure.
Bistro into Cheetah.
Feeling giddy and

positively apostatic
at the clinic, the perfect
little heart-shaped heart
beneath '82 in this old
used copy of *Between
the Acts* gives affect to
my argument for connection
within. Child seats man
in rear. Dana, I'm going
to address this end to
you—I've just read
your piece on Geoff
and you, music and
that blurry opulence
the love of a particular
love's company induces
from future memories.
I'm in awe of those
elaborate movie-watching
games you and Sarah
play, envious of yr couch
and its ears. I like to

think I hate the movies,
but I felt kindly
manipulated by *Apollo*
13 late last night after
inhaling a little deep
ash in order to faze
the process of clipping
sentences from my latest
variation on retuning
the old consciousness.
I identify with the
missing sections in
Typing "Wild Speech."
I thought to go public
with the whole thing
in this period of weird
interior folly compelling
me to print without
sanction the works
that force me to lock
fate in the bathroom
and rap its sour puss

on the head when it tries

to flee without asking.

I'm nothing if not polite,

even in absentia.

Love, Anselm.

Published by Wave Books

www.wavepoetry.com

Wave Books titles are distributed to the trade by

Consortium Book Sales and Distribution

Phone: 800-283-3572 / SAN 631-760X

This title is available in limited edition

hardcover directly from the publisher

Library of Congress Cataloging-in-Publication Data

Berrigan, Anselm.

Notes from irrelevance / Anselm Berrigan. — 1st ed.

p. cm.

ISBN 978-1-933517-54-4 (alk. paper)

I. Title.

PS3602.E7635N68 2011

811'.6—dc22

2010052076

Designed by Quemadura

Printed in the United States of America

9 8 7 6 5 4 3 2 1

First Edition

Wave Books 029

Excerpts from drafts of *Notes from Irrelevance* have been published in *Zen Monster*, *Peacock Online Review*, *Poets and Artists*, the *All Small Caps Anthology 4*, *Boston Review*, and *Green Mountains Review*. Thanks to Brian Unger & Lewis Warsh, Sophie Sills, Didi Menendez, Jess Mynes, Timothy Donnelly, and Elizabeth Powell, respectively, for these publications. Thanks as well to Alex Abelson for the video of a reading from *NFI* for *Poeteevee.com*.

The author wishes to thank Karen Weiser, Dana Ward, John Coletti, Mom, Eddie, Joshua Beckman, Anthony McCann, Alli Warren, and Matvei Yankelevich for feedback and encouragement. Thanks also to everyone who unknowingly contributed to the materials contained herein.